For Abbie.

I am the **BOSS** of my house.

You should meet my followers.

They are actually my humans, but I call them my followers because they follow me around

ALL DAY!

They are completely OBSESSED with me!

All I want to do is SLEEEEEEEEEEEEEP!

Ok... I didn't mean that.
Let me rephrase that.
All I want to do is
EAT THEN SLEEP!

They never leave me alone!

They follow me around with their phones ALL day long. Do you know how many pictures they take of me each day?

It's CRAZY!

If I bark at the TV, SNAP!

If my lip gets stuck in my teeth and suddenly I look like Elvis, SNAP!

Even if I don't move a muscle and just stare at them,

SNAP SNAP SNAP!

I can't shake these people!

Oh, and don't bother sneezing in their face,
that doesn't work!

They will laugh, squeeze and kiss you more
and harder than before!

For some reason, they think it's

HILARIOUS!

No wonder why my eyes are bulging out of my head!

I'm constantly getting

SQUEEEEEEZED!!!

On that note, they are complete suckers for my ♡ EYES ♡

My BIG, BROWN, BEAUTIFUL, BULGING eyes do have so many advantages!

I can practically get away with ANYTHING

as long as I look up at them with my big, glossy, browns!

They simply can't get enough of me!

They even go as far as spreading pieces of my hair

EVERYWHERE!

It's all over their furniture and clothes!

It's like they are worried they will forget
what I look or smell like or something!

In fact, I'm getting kind of worried about
them and their obsession over me...

Yes, I get it.

I am absolutely adorable and who couldn't love my fluffy squished face?

My ears are velvety soft and they glamorously bounce when I walk.

Have you checked out my tail?

It is perfect with a natural curl as if I walked straight out of the puppy spa.

I'm sure you've also noticed my confidence...

I will challenge ANYTHING no matter the size!

I don't mean to brag, but these are the facts!

Being so popular does have its downfalls.

I am forming SO many rolls that I think I've lost count!
I think it's because I do so many AMAZING
things all day and get rewarded for them!

You know, like when I'm sitting
still, looking out a window,
trying to sleep, looking bored, or
pretty much anything else I do!

Do you know any other dogs that get
treats for doing absolutely NOTHING???

Plus I can't say no, that would just be rude!

Since we're on the topic, did I mention how they scream and cheer when I go outside for a piddle?

I mean, there are other dogs that can see and hear you!!!

How EMBARRASSING!!!

So, I quickly shake a leg, do a dance, throw some grass, sneeze and play it off like I did something on purpose.

It's so HUMILIATING!

They're also always commenting on how I...

How should I say...

Leave traces of my "fragrances" behind.

I won't comment on that subject, just refer back to the excessive, yet well-deserved TREATS I mentioned before...

Again, not my fault!

That's another thing!

For some reason, turning my head back and forth when they talk to me is considered

"HILARIOUS"

They'll whip their phones out so fast and repeatedly ask me if I want to go for a walk, get a treat, or go potty!

I'm just trying to be a good listener!

THAT'S ALL!

Which reminds me.

You should hear them talk about how I "bring down the walls" when I sleep.

Snoring is only proof of a good nights sleep!

Have you ever heard of beauty rest?

Beauty takes WORK!

If that's what it takes to get it, SO BE IT!

Lastly, I hesitate to mention the most embarrassing part!

So embarrassing, that I can hardly bring myself to mention it!

Have **you** ever seen a pug in

CLOTHES???

Why is this SO amusing to humans?

Do I look amused? Pffff...

It's apparently part of my job description though, and it makes them happy, so I'll go along with it.

However, the look on my face should be obvious by now...

Wait...

What's that SOUND???

My followers are

HOME!

Yessssss! Finally!

This is the BEST part of my day!

They SQUEEZE and KISS me

and SWIRL me around the room!

As I look up at them with my big brown eyes, I can always count on seeing their

BIG SMILES

and

HAPPY FACES

looking down at me.